JAZPER

BY RICHARD EGIELSKI

A Laura Geringer Book

An Imprint of HarperCollinsPublishers

Jazper

Copyright © 1998 by Richard Egielski

Printed in the U.S.A. All rights reserved.

http://www.harperchildrens.com

Library of Congress Cataloging-in-Publication Data

Egielski, Richard.

Jazper / by Richard Egielski.

p.   cm.

"A Laura Geringer book."

Summary: While watching a house for five menacing moths, Jaz, an industrious young
bug, teaches himself how to transform into various other things and then must use this
talent to save himself.

ISBN 0-06-027817-X. – ISBN 0-06-027999-0 (lib. bdg.)

[1. Insects–Fiction.   2. Magic–Fiction.   3. Fathers and sons–Fiction.]   I. Title.

PZ7.E3215JAz 1998   97-32556

[E]–dc21   CIP

                                                                        AC

Typography by Alicia Mikles

1   2   3   4   5   6   7   8   9   10

First Edition

For Ian

Jazper and his dad lived together in a rented eggshell on the south side of Bugtown. Jazper loved to read. Every evening, before bed, he would read his dad a story.

"That's a good one, Jaz," his dad said. "I like the part where the frog blows up."

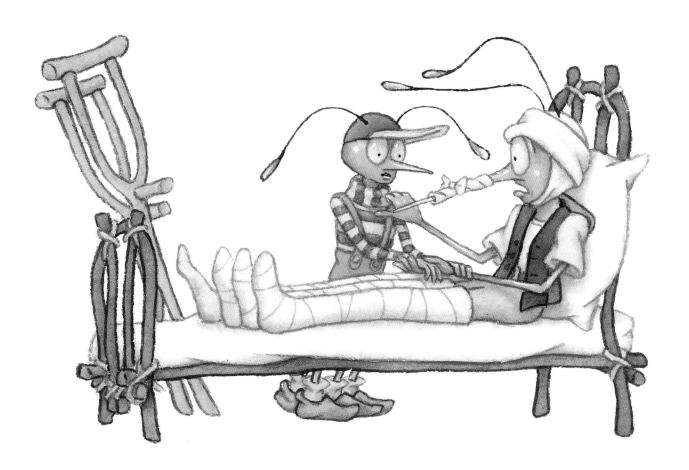

One afternoon, Jazper came home and found his dad
lying in bed with plaster casts on three of his legs and bandages
on his head.

"Dad! What happened?"

"There was an accident at the tomato plant," moaned his
dad. "I'll be out of work for weeks. Oh, how will we pay the rent?"

"Don't worry, Dad," said Jazper. "I'll get a job! We'll be
all right, you'll see."

The next morning Jazper woke up early. He got dressed,
fixed breakfast for his dad, packed himself a lunch, and
headed uptown to seek his fortune.

HELP
WANTED

It wasn't too long before Jazper spotted a HELP WANTED sign and five weird moths.

"You clean and watch the house for three weeks," they said.

"But my dad . . ."

"Yes or no!" they demanded.

". . . Yes," Jazper said. So the moths took off.

Jazper called his dad to tell him about the job. Then he settled in.

In the morning he swept the floor. In the afternoon he dusted. Jazper missed his dad, especially at night. So every night he read a book or two. They were books of tricks and magic.

Exactly at the end of three weeks, the moths returned. They paid Jazper and sent him on his way. He ran all the way home.

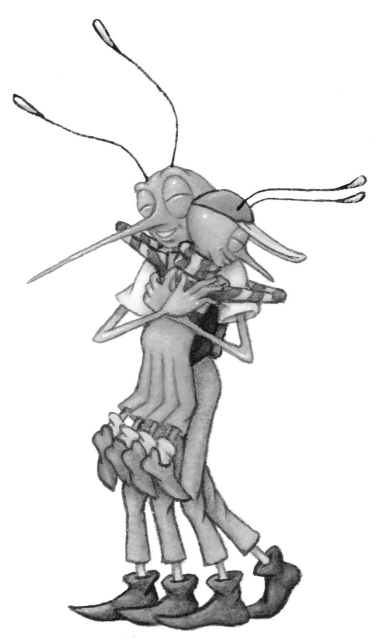

"Dad! Dad! Look what I can do!" Jazper said as he turned himself into a cheese doodle.

"Jaz? Wha . . . ?" His dad was confused.

"Come on, Dad. It'll be terrific. We'll make millions. You'll see."

Calling himself the Amazing Jazper, he performed feats of magic transformation.

He was an instant success. Crowds gathered.

He got a great write-up in the newspaper.

When the moths found out about Jazper, they went berserk.

"He read our books! He does our tricks!" they howled. "We'll fix him!"

Jazper was performing his popular sour pickle when the moths showed up . . .

and turned themselves into five slicing knives!

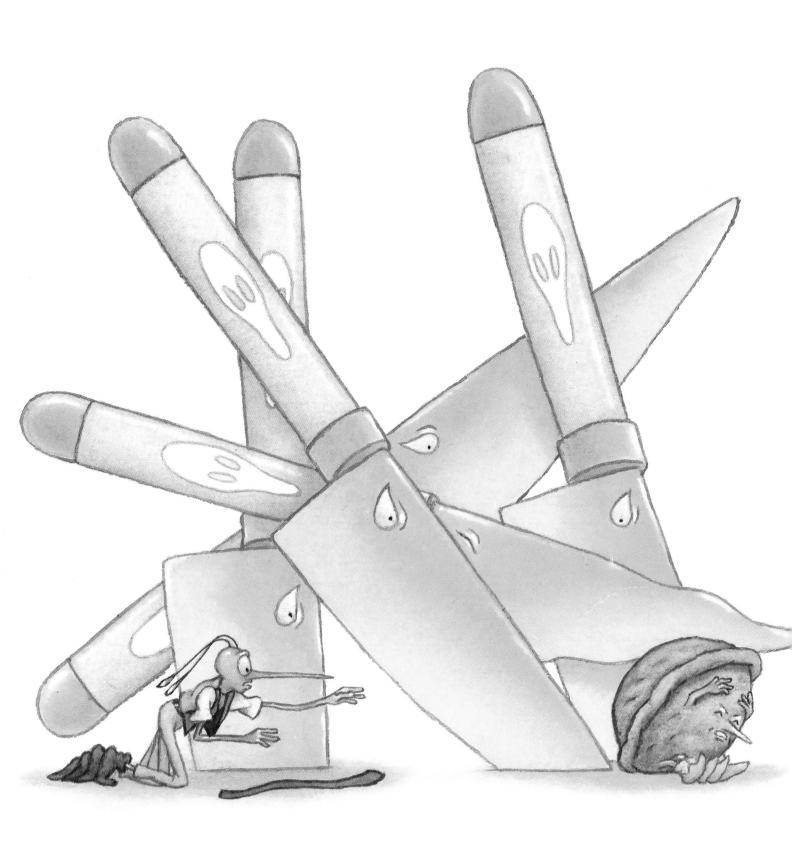

Just in time, Jazper turned into a hard nut.

So they turned into five fierce nutcrackers.

To escape, Jazper turned into a paper airplane.

So they turned into five burning flames.

Instantly, before they could think, Jazper turned into a
rain cloud and put out the flames.

"Noooooooooo . . ." they hissed, and were gone!

Exhausted, Jazper collapsed.

"Jaz? Are you all right?" his dad cried.

Jazper nodded. "Dad," he said, "I just thought of something else I could turn into, a . . ."

"Jaz. I would really like it if you just stayed yourself for a while."

So he did.